NURSERY CRIMES

ARTHUR GEISERT

HOUGHTON MIFFLIN COMPANY BOSTON

WALTER LORRAINE BOOKS

For Bonnie

Walter Lorraine *wl* Books

www.houghtonmifflinbooks.com

Library of Congress Cataloging-in-Publication Data
Geisert, Arthur.
    Nursery crimes / by Arthur Geisert.
        p. cm.
    Summary: For Thanksgiving Day, the fourteen pigs in the Jambonneau
family trim their trees to look like turkeys, but wake up one morning to find
they have all been stolen.
    RNF ISBN 0-618-06487-7   PA ISBN 0-618-95671-9
    [1. Trees—Fiction. 2. Farms—Fiction. 3. Robbers and outlaws—Fiction.
4. Pigs—Fiction. 5. Thanksgiving Day—Fiction.] I. Title.

PZ7.G2724 Nu 2001
[E]—dc21   00-059740
                                                                            CIP

RNF ISBN-13: 978-0-618-06487-8
PA ISBN-13:   978-0-618-95671-5

Manufactured in China
SCP 10 9 8 7 6 5 4 3 2

Jambonneau and his pretty wife, Merville de Peru, immigrated from Amiens, France, to a small tree nursery just south of Ames, Iowa, an area famous for its tree nurseries. Jambo and Marva, as they were known in America, had twelve children. From an early age, the children were taught how to trim trees into sculptural shapes. They were skilled in the art of topiary. Jambo and Marva also dealt in giant pumpkins and salvage to make ends meet.

Every fall, all the nurseries in the area trimmed trees
into the shape of turkeys. There was a big demand for them.

The children were good topiarists. They loved their craft.
This afternoon, they were finishing the first turkeys of the year.

Jambo was the first one awake the next morning. When he
went outside to stretch, he saw that the turkeys were gone!

Not a single topiary was left.

"We've been robbed! Everybody up!"

"Let's look for clues!"

They looked high and low.

They decided to follow some suspicious tracks.

The tracks led up the road to Voler's place.

Voler was a notorious topiary thief.

They climbed the fence.

They could not tell their turkeys from all the others
so the sheriff couldn't help.

Dinner that day was grim. Without the turkey money,
they would have a very hard time this winter.

"We'll be all right," Marva said. "We'll make some more.
Get your tools, and I'll pick the trees to work on."

The children worked like beavers.

Meanwhile, Jambo and Marva devised a plan.
They hollowed out some pumpkins.

That night Jambo and Marva kept watch on their turkeys.

And inside each pumpkin was a little topiarist.

The next morning, they found that they had been robbed again.
Everyone had been so tired that they had fallen asleep.

It looked like Voler's work. He was always suspected
when topiaries were missing, but nothing was ever proven.

After the exhausted kids had gone to bed, Marva and
Jambo had coffee in the kitchen. "We're ruined," Jambo said.
"Maybe not," Marva replied with a smile.

"Look at the temperature, Jambo. It's 24 degrees. Our
first hard frost," Marva said. "Call the sheriff and wake the
children. We're going to Voler's."

"Those are our turkeys," Marva said, pointing to the yellow ones. Marva had selected some special trees for their latest turkeys. Unlike the evergreen topiary, they changed color in fall.

The yellow turkeys were a complete surprise to Voler.
The sheriff was happy because now he could finally pin
something on the topiary thief.

The sheriff arrested Voler and his men and took them off to jail.

Voler confessed to everything. All the turkeys were
returned to their owners.

Later that fall, Jambo and Marva had a big sale. By then, the
turkeys were really turkey-colored. They sold right away.

They sold their pumpkins, too. They treated everyone
to apples, corn, cider, and cookies.

Over time, Jambo and Marva's turkeys became famous
at Thanksgiving, and their business prospered.